The Gift

T0344640

Florence Noiville

The Gift

A Novel

TRANSLATED FROM THE FRENCH BY
Catherine Temerson

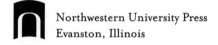 Northwestern University Press
Evanston, Illinois

Northwestern University Press
www.nupress.northwestern.edu

Printed in the United States of America

10 9 8 7 6 5 4 3 2 1

This is a work of fiction. Characters, places, and events are the product
of the author's imagination or are used fictitiously and do not represent
actual people, places, or events.

Library of Congress Cataloging-in-Publication Data

Noiville, Florence.
    [Donation. English]
    The gift / Florence Noiville ; translated from the French by Catherine
Temerson.
        p. cm.
    ISBN 978-0-8101-2676-3 (cloth : alk. paper)
    1. Manic-depressive illness—Fiction. 2. Mothers and daughters—Fiction.
I. Temerson, Catherine. II. Title.
PQ2714.O48D6613 2012
843.92—dc23

                                                           2011051525

∞ The paper used in this publication meets the minimum requirements
of the American National Standard for Information Sciences—Permanence
of Paper for Printed Library Materials, ANSI Z39.48-1992.

To my mother,

and for my daughters

Nothing can save us.
Nor can anything be our undoing either.
—FÉNELON

Do not laugh; do not weep. Understand.
—SPINOZA

CONTENTS

The Gift

We are all orphans. Our need for consolation is insatiable.

I was ten years old when I lost my parents. They're both in fine shape today, but I keep moving heaven and earth to recapture something of the life from before. I can't pinpoint what exactly. I'm looking for the original bedrock. A trace from before the world was turned upside down.

Dear Parents

The idea of writing to them came to me when I was at the station. I had just missed the 11:57 train from Tours to Paris, a ghost train that I was convinced I had seen on the schedule. But the man at the ticket window assured me that it didn't exist. I twisted and turned the handle of my purse. I don't like being wrong. What else could I do but sit down at the station buffet and wait for the next train, one that would be less virtual? There was a golden quality to the air. The russet color of autumn in the Val-de-Loire. A balmy respite before winter.

The last light, the last glow, echoing my feelings during the entire trip to my parents' house, and it wrung my heart.

It must have been obvious. On the way to the station, in the car, my mother was worried. I looked dispirited. "No, really." I was angry with myself for not finding the words that would have soothed her, for she was always so tormented. I felt that, on this day particularly, a display of joyful gratitude and absolute contentment was called for. As usual, I was not up to it. As usual, I was angry with myself.

Write to them. Yes. Writing to them would make up for this failing. I rummaged through my purse for a pen and a piece of paper. Waited for my tea to be served. Wanted to start—but how? "Dear parents," cold and formal. "Dear Papa, Dear Mama," childish, almost inane. I wondered what Kafka's opening words were in his *Letter to His Father*. I thought of Singer, a prolific writer yet unable to pen a single line to his mother. I made up a thousand excuses to persuade myself that writing to one's parents, even at forty plus, was a much more perilous exercise than people thought.

When I looked up for inspiration, I saw, on the wall of the station, five big letters painted in black: T O U R S. They stood out individually, like at the ophthalmologist's. Or like on a death announcement. They were carved in the tufa, the stone of the châteaux, a limestone that gets whiter and silkier as it ages. I thought of my mother's hair, so very white. I told myself that what I had to say to them in this letter wasn't all that hard to express. I had to thank them for the gift they had just made to us, to my sister and me. Thank them for being the people they had become and for growing lovelier, in a way, both of them, with time, just like the tufa in fact. Which was also a way of making up with them, after so many years of misunderstandings and conflicts.

The tea was cold. I picked up my pen again. Jotted down three or four sentences, but crossed them out as soon as they were written. Inadequate. Inhibited. The letter didn't have to be perfect. It just had to be true. It just had to be me. That was the whole problem. I thought: I'm a bag of knots, miles of rope tied up in knots and crammed together, *encramillés*. (*Encramillé* is a word used by my grandmother from the Ardennes. It's patois from

Charleville or Sedan. You won't find it in any dictionary but its mere utterance conveys the inextricable aspect of things.) This silence, it occurred to me, would be interpreted once again as lack of emotion; at this thought, a kind of rage and desperation welled up in me.

This was when they announced train number 3545 bound for Paris, making stops in Blois, Mer, Beaugency, Meung-sur-Loire, and Orléans. Usually this string of names reminded me of the old song "Orléans, Beaugency, Notre-Dame-de-Cléry, Vendôme . . ."

But this time my heart wasn't in it. I grabbed my belongings—my bag weighed down by sedums and quince jelly—and, with a persistent feeling of emptiness and guilt, I headed to the platform.

Bare Owner

The day before, we had all met at the lawyer's—my parents, my sister, and I—for the settlement of a gift. This was a few kilometers from Tours, a tiny community—the village where I had grown up, in a huge house with a tower, grounds, a poplar grove, horses, and, to top it all off, a river.

We said, "Bonjour, Maître," and sat down, the four of us, in slightly worn armchairs. The deed was waiting for us on the green leather of the desk. And the lawyer, with a good-natured expression, started to give us a reading of it:

"THE YEAR TWO THOUSAND FIVE

"AUGUST TWENTY-FIFTH

"Maître H. was given the present authentic deed, containing a gift in anticipation of a shared estate at the request of the persons designated hereinafter.

"PARTIES TO THE DEED . . ."

Then came the enumeration of the above-named parties purported to be "of age and competent" for the "execution of the present will and its consequences."

Had I already tuned out at that point? I don't think so. The lawyer spoke in a low, confident voice. I remember being amused by the slightly quaint vocabulary surrounding this exchange *inter vivos*. Even the assessment of the "portion of estate of which testator may dispose" didn't put me off. Yet there was definitely a moment when I suddenly saw everything cast in another light. Thinking about it again it was probably inevitable. The man was talking about the "surviving donor" and the "death of the predeceased." At times he broke off and I had the feeling he was looking specifically at us, at my sister and me, to make sure he wasn't going too fast. Underlying these pauses was a single expectation, which kept recurring, the moment when "usufruct and bare ownership" would be reconciled. I understood that he meant to say: the day when both your parents will be dead.

But why was he going to such lengths to use convoluted phrases for something so simple and terrifying? And why did "possession"—my sister's and mine—have to take effect precisely "from that day on"?

It was at that point that my thoughts began to run riot and follow their own course. I suppose that the transfer from one generation to the next, which includes, implicitly, the idea of our parents' death, quite naturally brings us face to face with our own. Or else, which amounts to the same thing, leads us to reread our own life *as seen by them*. Is this why everything resurfaced at that very moment? Some people see their life flash by just before death. Others when they're at the analyst's. For me, it was in a lawyer's office that I suddenly thought I understood everything. In terms of what he called the "cessions" and "required divestitures" to become a "bare owner."

For me "owner" was a strange word. "Bare," much less so. Reasonably or unreasonably I had always seen myself as lonely and bare—uprooted. Later, in writing this book, I understood why the gift had reawakened it all. Everything revolved around it. The gift, with all its variations: gift, give, forgive, forsake. And vice versa.

3

"Switzerland Is a Beautiful Country, You'll See"

One of my most painful childhood memories. I'm standing on the platform of a train station—yet another station. I'm ten years old. Blue coat, blue eyes, and blond hair, carefully parted and braided on each side of my head. The braids are not as meticulously and tightly plaited as when my mother does my hair; then not a single hair sticks out. She likes "neat and tidy" children. On that day, I'm alone with my father. I'm about to take the train to Lausanne. The Trans-Europe Express or "TEE," Papa said, squeezing my hand. He injected a hint of admiration in his voice meant to imply:

"You'll be traveling alone in that famous train. Do you realize that even at my age I haven't taken it yet?"

Actually, all he said was:

"Switzerland is a beautiful country, you'll see."

At that particular moment, I know that he couldn't care less about the Engadine and the Grisons. He's forcing himself to say that. He's uncomfortable too. I nod in response. Don't talk. Don't burst into tears. Don't show how frightened you are. Don't betray your feelings. Subsequently, I understood that above all I was struggling not to let him down.

Once again, Mama was in the middle of an acute nervous breakdown. *Depression, manic-depressive, bipolar, psychosis, psychiatric clinic*—these words were never uttered at home, but children know everything. During a previous "episode," in which my mother had to be rushed to the hospital, my grandmother had looked after my sister and me, in the Ardennes. Images come back to me from that vacation, or rather from that vacant state. I'm with her (my grandmother) in the rows of gooseberry bushes, at the far end of the garden. The gooseberries offer themselves up to us with their thick pearly skin and tiny shaggy bristles. Their colors are very subtle like a necklace of fine pearls, ranging from creamy white to delicate pink. There are also the big crimson berries that turn into a purée when you bite into them.

Trying to sound as innocent as possible, I say to my grandmother, "Do you think Mama's going to die?" She wipes away a tear, very discreetly. I know my mother isn't going to die. I just want someone to talk to me.

Freud tells the story of a child who is forced to stay in the dark. I've forgotten the circumstances. No doubt he's been punished and locked inside a closet. The child wants someone to talk to him. "That won't change anything," the adult replies, "you'll still be in the dark." The child: "There's more light in the dark when someone talks to you."

The Secret of Secrets

There's a feeling of loss, of being uprooted. A mystery too, the idea that the "secret of secrets" will have to be deciphered. Because my mother's sudden disappearance shows that there is no *given*. And especially, above all, that in a single instant, everything can sway, turn upside down, crumble, shatter into smithereens, disintegrate into dust. The words that come to me are in English: "fall apart," "fall to pieces" . . . (My friend Eva, who is American and very "think positive," points out that basing one's life on that premise is not necessarily proof of pessimism. "You can only be pleasantly surprised.")

Constant insecurity. I'm ten years old and have only one certainty: at every step, the ground can shake. There's the threat of collapse. The earth's crust is just a crust, in fact, a "coat of skin," a "cortex" (*scortea* in Latin), and this membrane, much more fragile than it appears, is also the outside shell, the misleading, enticing stratum of surface appearance.

Yet when I think back on the gooseberry bushes, even today I still wonder about the touch of perversity in my question to my grandmother. As young as I was, I was able to unsettle such a strong woman with just a few words. I was a victim but I had power as well. I was the child of a sick mother. Different. If I make an effort to be completely honest I'm not sure that I didn't *also* take advantage of this difference. The kind of painful pride that comes with the feeling of being "special."

I'm Hopeless

Yet on that day, on the train to Lausanne, I'm not feeling very confident. These aristocrats, these friends of my parents with whom I'm being sent to live for the summer, are people I hardly know. I'm frightened. Frightened of the separation, the void, the wrenching severance. The ten-year-old child's fear equals the fear of the forty-year-old child. They say that abandonment is the primal trauma. The one that leaves its mark on the rest of a person's life. Birth, separation, cutting the umbilical cord, weaning . . . Father, father, why have you forsaken me?

My father is completely absorbed by the state of his wife's health. Trying to be there for me and yet unavailable. Absent to me as well as to himself. It's not his fault.

My mother is in the hospital, it's not her fault either, but she has left us; that's a fact. For how long? For what reason? What illness plagues her? To all these questions, the adults provide only evasive answers. I'll have to figure it out on my own. My conclusion is that we, her children, are not an adequate source of joy and love to compensate for the all-consuming sadness that engulfs her. Our presence on earth is not enough. Not *for her*. This is an idea that infuriates me. I'm ten years old; I'd like to be the sun around which everything revolves. I'd like to be at the center and I'm merely at the periphery, a foreign body, perhaps even a nuisance since I have to be sent away so serious matters can be attended to.

Unless—and this hypothesis is even more destabilizing—unless it all comes from me. Because I'm not strong enough, not funny enough, not amazing enough, not gifted enough to pull this mother away from the abyss that is sucking her in. Everything is my fault. A buried guilt preys on me. I'm hopeless. It's a leitmotif. A feeling that will haunt us, my sister and me.

Does the gift include that as well? The transfer of the gene of doubt. Of self-doubt, spinning out of control. I've always wondered about this grim heritage. I've often wanted to read a serious study on the psychology of children whose mothers were bipolar. Perhaps the children remain forever imprinted by this unusual interweaving of insouciance and gravity. As though life were a mere "smile on the lips of death." I think this image just happens to come from a Swiss poet (Cingria?). Switzerland is a beautiful country.

6

E Pericoloso Sporgersi

My father made my presence known to the ticket collector. He left me in the care of a "respectable-looking" woman. He went to buy me something to eat and gave me money—too much money. He checked that I knew the train's arrival time, that my watch hadn't stopped, that my car number matched the one he had initially recorded and given to Mrs. de F., who would be waiting for me on the platform in Lausanne. He did everything perfectly. Everything I would do myself, today, for my own children. Yet I felt he was multiplying these tasks to fill the void that was gripping us as the hour of departure approached. I was fully aware that he looked as forlorn as I did. He joked, as usual. But I sensed that the same powerless anguish flowed in our veins. We inherit the texture of our hair or the shape of our fingers, why couldn't we also inherit our parents' unspoken anxieties? The two of us were haunted by one and only one question: what would happen afterward?

Afterward, I decided that I had to help him. That I shouldn't be another problem for him. He was the brooding widower, aggrieved, disconsolate. The last thing he needed was someone adding to his worries. It was best to be self-effacing and forgotten. I began to make myself unobtrusive, tiptoeing my way around. This is how one becomes the top student in the class. The impetus was neither pride nor ambition, but necessity. I brought home unimpeachable report cards. My long hair would be stroked; I would be congratulated; then it was on to the next thing. I was left in peace, which I didn't mind at all. And more importantly, I left them in peace, the two of them, alone with their problems. I would melt into the background; hold my breath; struggle and strain not to speak. It was my way of helping—stop breathing, erase my presence. At the time I saw no other way. No noticeable difficulty, nothing worthy of reproach: I was a good child and a good student. Hunched up, tiny, in a corner of the picture. Nothing protruded. *E pericoloso sporgersi:* Danger! Do not lean out.

Because Nothing Could Be Done About It

I don't remember the arrival in Lausanne. Nor do I recall much about the stay in Switzerland, in Crans-sur-Sierre. Only a few scattered pictures come to mind. A picnic in the clouds, with a guide from the Valais—it's the first time I taste raclette cheese, which was not yet popular in France. Mr. de F's strong-smelling, peppery eau de toilette. A curling match I was taken to . . . It occurs to me, thinking back on it, that it must have been a very chic vacation, but I didn't realize it at the time. Did I cry at night, silently, into my pillow? I was ill at ease. I pretended to be cheerful—that I remember very clearly. Acted as though I didn't have a lump of anxiety in my throat. Make believe, have guts, keep up appearances—the great struggle.

Afterward, I returned to France. We were supposed to spend the end of the summer in Cannes, all together. I had to take a plane and meet my parents at the Nice airport. (Still the same apprehension, still traveling all by myself, and feigning, once again, that I could handle it like a pro. Later I imposed the same thing on my daughters. Trains, planes, ships, between England and France, between Greece and France, nothing was to stop them. They managed without mishaps and even with apparent ease. Was I wrong? I wanted them to be independent and strong. Stronger than me? But maybe they felt that same lump of anxiety in their throats? Maybe they didn't dare complain? The idea comes to mind that battered parents make battered children, I mean children that they can't help battering in turn. Was I acting on the—cruel?—temptation of making them realize that you travel alone your whole life? And that this should be understood as early as possible? Was this arming them or disarming them? I may have been wrong to ask all this of them.)

The arrival in Nice. There they are. Close together, leaning on a guardrail, in the area where you wait for passengers. I have the vague impression that they're looking down at me—that's it, the guardrail is high up, outside, in the sunshine. Whereas I'm down below with my suitcase, I have to look up to see them and they signal to me. I don't know why I'm struck by this detail.

Seeing them together . . . Papa looking happy, his pale blue eyes, his smile. My mother . . . She is wearing a yellow and pink silk dress with an off-the-shoulders neckline and a bow in the back. It should look elegant on a brunette. But she is not the same. She has become dreadfully fat. I don't recognize her. She tries to smile. And me too, I have to try to smile back: it's the long-awaited day, the day when she has left the psychiatric clinic and is with us at last. But it isn't her. I feel like screaming. A woman so beautiful, so slender, so elegant. The sight of this disaster makes me want to yell. Smash everything. Why does she look like this, all fat and puffy? Even her arms and shoulders, which used to be so graceful, are deformed. I look for the little bone that used to protrude from her summer dresses and for the perfect nape of her neck. I'm angry at her. I can't help being angry at her.

My mother was gone, I missed her terribly but my image of her had remained intact. I still had something left; I still had her beauty. And now the woman I got back was fat; she had become ugly. Everything had been ruined and trampled on. Today this impulsive and selfish reaction surprises me. Yet I can still feel the violent rage that arose in me then. *Even the image* of my mother had been shattered and this was unbearable.

They must have noticed the anger in my eyes. Very quickly, as best they could, they explained to me—she herself may even have done it, it could not have been easy for her either, the distorting mirror her daughter held up to her—they explained to me that the medication, in these cases, caused one to get terribly fat, and that nothing could be done about it.

Nothing could be done about it.

Such Slender Limbs

I'm not idealizing her. She was truly beautiful. The epitome of charm and grace. My friends (and boyfriends) remarked on it often enough. It used to amuse me. I don't remember being in the least jealous of her, instead I was proud. This was not where hostility, incomprehension, misunderstandings lay. At seventeen, I was in love with a man who was thirty years my senior. He had been my literature teacher. A surrogate father. I loved no one else. You could say that the others were there like a court of beaux whose sole purpose was to reassure me about myself. It was fun, at home, to see these young men mooning over me, over her, or over the two of us simultaneously. This was years after the return from Nice and she long since had shed her unwanted pounds and recovered what we in the family called, not without envy, her "hourglass figure" and "slender limbs."

In photos, she reminded me of Sophia Loren. Piazza San

Marco, in the late fifties, she is feeding the pigeons, arms outstretched. A silk chiffon scarf is tied around her Madonna-like face. During the same period she is in Paris wearing a polka-dot dress. A ringlet of black hair graces her forehead, she is fastening her earring—she must be getting ready to go out. A year earlier, in the Lérins Islands, she is stretched out in a rocky inlet wearing a white bikini, perfect bustline, perfect figure. (This all dates from before I was born. I like this series of photos where my father is present too. I almost feel that by staring at the image I'll be able to step into it and walk on the seaweed carpet in Sainte-Marguerite, this flat, incredibly smooth and silky seaweed that clings to the feet and ankles . . .)

On the following page, truth be told, she is posing a bit and acting coquettish. ("Oh dear, that's me!" she'll later say to her sons-in-law, pretending to come upon these photos by accident while looking for those of her daughters.) I prefer her in Juan-les-Pins where we see her waterskiing, raising an arm or a leg, looking very relaxed behind her father's Chris-Craft—these shots are signed by a professional local photographer, maybe because water skiing was a sport few women pursued at the time?

Not the slightest attempt, in any case, to avoid the lens. In every picture, she is smiling and looking directly at the camera. You would search in vain for a trace of sadness, a warning sign of melancholy. Not a hint of "social phobia." Is she posing? Is she forcing herself? Every time I look at them, these photos add to my perplexity. I've always wondered where, when, and how everything suddenly cracked.

Deed of Damnation

"This deed of donation is expressly agreed to and accepted by the DONATORS and DONEES, as stated above . . ."

I give a start. Apparently the lawyer had addressed me. He is waiting for a name, a number, an answer. I'm angry at myself for having drifted off, as I often do, into a kind of absent meditation. I try to recall his last sentence. Was I dreaming? Did he say deed of donation? I heard deed of damnation. "With the obligation of the beneficiaries to incorporate in the present deed of damnation under section 1078-1 of the Civil Code as per conditions indicated," etc. It's absurd. It all becomes muddled. How did I manage to escape from these padded walls and land on the Riviera? And why is the image of my youngest daughter, L., who turned ten today, suddenly superimposed on my recollection of my mother?

If I Told You . . .

The carefree days of childhood: *enfance/insouciance*. An easy, lazy-man's rhyme. Appealing but appalling. Fully conscious of my limitations, for all of my ten years I tried to protect my parents. This obvious fact hit me one day when I was taking L., who was very little, to an analyst. She had developed a phobia of rubber balloons and the noise they made when they burst. A phobia that had eventually included celebrations, birthday parties, children's tea parties, and which threatened to turn into agoraphobia.

One day while I was looking for a parking space on the rue des Beaux-Arts, I—foolishly—encouraged her to talk to me. What was it about balloons that frightened her so much? "I can't tell you," she said coolly. Her voice was measured. Her words detached. Every little silence was like a mountain crevasse, a fault that had to be jumped over with concentration to avoid falling into the seemingly bottomless icy hole. I asked her why and she replied, "If I told you, it would make you cry." Then she said nothing; the discussion was over.

So it was her turn, she was protecting me; she was becoming her mother's mother. Just as I had felt like a mother and no longer a child the day I took the train to Lausanne. There was a jolt. I parked badly, rue des Beaux-Arts, and rammed into the fender of the car behind us. Was it me who had passed on to her this oppressive sense of responsibility? This unconscious legacy, this genetic burden? Just as we can be bequeathed land or a business, is it possible to inherit what physicians call a "depression-prone" breeding ground? And what can ever blossom on this black breeding ground? It seemed to me that we were prisoners fettered by buried chains—the shackles of *malesserre*, as the Italians say. Something from the past was being replayed within us. And was playing with us, tossing us up in the air like rag dolls, and letting us drop down, inert and battered.

In the waiting room, I don't know why, I recalled Medea slitting her children's throats—a scene pictured on a small red amphora in my parents' bookcase. My grandfather, a Hellenist, had brought it back years ago from an excavation site at Cape Sounion. As a child, I used to sneak in to look at it in secret. Was this idea of inexorable repetition already in my mind in some vague way? Later—I was probably fifteen or so—Bergman's film *Autumn Sonata* had made a great impression on me. It was playing in the fashionable Tours movie theater, an auditorium built in the 1970s with roughcast walls and orange seats. Somewhere I must still have the small notebook with the elastic fastener in which I had neatly jotted down this sentence: "Mother and daughter, what a horrible, dreadful combination of helplessness, emotion, and destruction. In the name of solicitude, affection, and love anything is possible. The mother's flaw will be the daughter's flaw. The daughter will pay for the mother's failings. The mother's misfortune will be the daughter's misfortune. It's as though the umbilical cord had never been cut."

Damnation. Is there no other solution but to live through, for, or against our parents? I would like to assess the ineluctable nature of that idea, but my thoughts slip away. My memory of the film is mixed with that of the theater. Everything is intertwined, the contrast between the harsh roughness of the walls and the velvet springiness of the seats. The solemn and awkward piano prelude—well, I think it's a prelude—that Liv Ullmann plays for Ingrid Bergman. I see a parallel with the sketch a little girl hands to her mother desperately seeking approval. (Or with this book, which, if you think about it, may be nothing more than an elaborate first doodle, a portrait of her, intended for her . . .)

Actually isn't the life of a daughter just that—a sketch offered apprehensively to her mother? In response to which all she gets is the fixed, polite, damning smile of the sublime Ingrid?

Life from the Past

I've never ceased to be amazed by the life from the past that persists within us. Even as newborns, my daughters, it seemed, were always more mature and wiser than I. As though they *knew* from the day of their birth. And were still haunted by distant ancestors. The mark of disquiet was hidden in the depths of their beings. They were the repositories of a history—an aggregate of wounds, allusions, and secrets had settled, like sediment, inside them. As though each of us passed down to our descendants tiny particles of a "truth" fated to find a repository later in other bodies.

At nightfall my daughters would start to cry, for no apparent reason. Pediatricians call it vespertine anxiety. An imprecise, convenient label. I thought I heard the moans of all the successive generations of the family living inside them, living inside us, squabbling, mangling one another, tearing one another apart, the great commotion of the dead and the living. It was hard for me to put up with these cries. I would call Stefa, my best friend.

Stefa is of Czech descent. She's a pediatrician in a big Paris hospital. I can still hear her sigh as she reiterated the things she had told me a hundred times. "Stop worrying. It's all very simple." Simple? "Yes . . . Just remember your daughter is a small defense-less mammal. Her nervous system isn't fully developed, you see, and she's intuitively aware of how vulnerable she is. She *knows* that if no one takes care of her, she won't survive. Deep down, this is a certainty we all share, even symbolically. We know that if our mothers don't take care of us as children, we'll die. Imagine the fears this can lead to: the anxiety of being abandoned, of hun-ger, of cold, of death . . ."

I object. I explain that I take care of L. all the time. That I even stopped working, temporarily, to be with her. Whereas she's been crying for three quarters of an hour for no apparent reason, and this is how it's been every day. Every day at exactly 6:30 p.m., if you really want to know.

Stefa seems reassuring: I can't satisfy all of L.'s needs. Even given all my tenderness, this little girl can still feel sadness and resentment.

I don't know what to say. I'm afraid of being a nuisance. She adds that in any case it's pointless for me to give in to melancholy. "Don't forget that babies communicate from unconscious to un-conscious, as the psychiatrists say. L. is like a seismograph. She records the tiniest change in your mental landscape. Though she doesn't talk, she feels and interprets. You know, it's something you read everywhere, the subconscious of a child is a sponge . . ."

"You mean it's my fault if she cries?"

"Stop, with your faults. It's not about blame."

I change the subject and ask if she's heard from H., the tall, dark young man I saw at her house the other evening. She tells me that her love life, alas, is a fiasco. I suggest we have lunch together and discuss it. We agree to phone each other again for, as it happens, she's expecting a phone call.

I think: my daughter is calling me and I can't respond. Stefa is expecting a call that won't come. Is someone trying to tell us something?

Still Face

If our mothers don't take care of us as children, we die. For a long time, Stefa's sentence remained coiled up in my head—like a nice little blindworm, harmless and motionless—and awakened no specific chord. It came back to me a short time ago. I had come across a newspaper article: "Every year in France 10 to 15% of new mothers suffer from depression, especially in the first three months after their baby's birth. This may have repercussions on the child's subsequent cognitive development." This item came from the fourth encephalon conference. (I didn't even know there were such things as encephalon conferences as there may also be colon symposiums or international meetings on zygomatic apophysis.) In short, during a plenary session devoted to children of parents with psychiatric disorders, Professor L., according to the author of the article, had stressed this "real public health problem so rarely recognized" and emphasized the importance of what is called—another thing I learned—the "tuning up of mother and child." At first I thought of a little violin looking for the A by the side of a fat old cello, or of a small chamber music group, when the players exchange glances before starting to play. Then I remembered Stefa's words: the mother notices the infant's emotions; her intonations, gestures, and smiles show the child that she has understood them. The child, in turn, knows that he or she has been "heard." All of this paves the way for the development of language.

But what happens when there is a "tuning problem"? The article mentioned video tests called "still face" tests. They showed just how much a child's reactions are influenced by the mother's psyche. "A six-month-old infant smiles, opens its eyes wide, shapes its lips into an 'O,' and tries to sit up if prompted by a well-adjusted mother. Conversely, a depressed, emotionally absent woman who expresses herself in a monotonous voice, will not succeed in arousing her baby's interest; her six-month-old infant will slump into its 'bouncer chair' half asleep."

A short time ago, my mother mentioned her postpartum depression for the first time in my presence. The childbirth had been difficult. Forceps. Unexpected complications. The physician had implied that it might not be possible to save both mother and child.

Choose between the two? I wonder what went through my father's head at that moment. (Actually I'd rather not wonder.) Be that as it may, what my mother emphasized was her deep despondency after the birth. She cried all the time; she had no milk; she felt guilty, frustrated, convinced she was a bad mother.

I can visualize this new mother's beautiful young face bathed in tears. *Mater dolorosa.* As an infant, what did I see in the mirror of her features? I'll never know. Perhaps it was like banging against a white wall (against which I would be banging all the time) because no interaction was possible, the person who should have been closest to me was elsewhere, infinitely distant because of her own mental suffering. Detached from her child and already, in the child's eyes, *incomprehensible*.

And what about me? Did I feel guilty in turn? Was I furious? Did I resent her for not being able to feed me?

"You used to give me nasty looks," she blurted out in the conversation. I shuddered. This sentence seemed incredibly violent to me.

"Do you really think an infant can give someone nasty looks?" I asked.

She didn't answer.

Vicious Circle

"Beauty, my dear concern." When I think of my mother, beauty and concern are inseparable. Was it the torment, the inner chaos that led her to being obsessed with order for its appeasing effect, with beauty for its calming influence? Or was it the other way around? Did her craving for perfection (richness, quietness, and pleasure), never satisfied, so frustrate her that it aroused anger and drama? Was all this impossible to disentangle? Submerged in the mysterious opaqueness of disease?

I would like to explore these questions without bias—as though it were possible. Try first to pull out the thread of beauty. She adored antique stores, flea markets, auction houses. She was passionately fond of antique rugs and furniture. Her taste was impeccable, she had a talent for tracking down antiques; made new things out of old; reupholstered chairs and armchairs; painted, framed, sewed, restored, mended, and tinkered . . . She knew how to do everything to create the Beautiful.

As a result, the house was all hers. With a museum-like, frozen quality. The large drawing room, the chests of drawers signed by famous cabinetmakers, the Aubusson tapestry, the collection of antique instruments, the Tang horse . . . these were not really meant for children. Nor for my sister and me as adolescents, nor, later, for my daughters—her granddaughters; my mother hated anyone sprawling out on sofas and feared incessantly for her art objects.

Their placement—and this was true throughout the house—had been decided on by her for once and for all. Just moving anything could upset her in a way that was unimaginable. "Each thing has its place, there is a place for each thing." It was final. Cleaning ladies never lasted long—they never did things "her way."

The garden was her kingdom. Her degree in pharmacology had made her an expert in botany. I saw her ironic smile at the Parisians who turned up (more and more infrequently) to spend weekends at our house. Confusing a willow and an alder, dear God, was that possible? Her closeness to nature was genuine. She made fun of incompetents who could only name a tree, a flower, or a bird generically. My friends got a proper dressing down. What was the use of knowing all the nuances of Althusser's or Spinoza's thought if you couldn't even distinguish between a water lily and a water flag? She lived *in the real world*. Not an intellectual but someone who sees and feels things. Who is joined to them.

And it was quite possible that things reassured her more than human beings. Because they do not betray us. They stand for us and are faithful to us—a faithfulness that is humble and silent. Hence the importance of the *gift*, which is not just the handing down of a legacy, but more importantly a way of putting property and objects in a safe place. For a mother, isn't giving her daughter an object that bears her mark an obvious way of living on?

Yet that's exactly when everything is cast in another light. And the need for beauty and harmony merges with the hell of everyday life. For beauty entailed a constant obligation. To renovate, repair, clean, oil, preserve, grease, maintain had become obsessions and even fixations. In her desire for perfection, my mother would draw up endless lists in her pointy handwriting, lists that were perpetually substituted one for the other:

- Sandpaper the fence
- Repaint the shutters
- Trim entrance box trees
- Cut virgin vine east wing
- Weed clump under American oaks
- Take out boat
- Unjam tower window
- Pick gooseberries
- Call roofer
- Call pruner pond poplar grove
- Stake up iris mixed border near bridge
- Bring in firewood kiosk
- Empty pavilion attic
- Replace slate tool shed
- Tidy up caretaker's house
- Weed under fig tree
- Repot agapanthus
- Etc.
- Etc.
- Etc.

The "garden" list was never ending, but the "house" list was just as long. Not to mention the other lists—professional, social—or the vacation list, for which the preparations were always an absolute nightmare. The lists: the "done" list, whose items were checked off with irate satisfaction; the "to-do" lists, things to bear in mind and to prepare, the reminders, the small scraps of paper, the Post-its . . . all those interminable lists akin to litanies of names on the monuments to the dead—what purpose did they serve? Are they written down in the way lines are scrawled in school, to fill up pages as a punishment? Are they sources of anxiety cast aside once articulated? Or, on the contrary, are they multiplied because nature abhors a vacuum? In the case of my mother, the last hypothesis was certainly the right one: all alone on a desert island, she would still have produced miles of lists.

Neither respite nor rest. Picking up a newspaper or a book during the day amounted to a loss of time. She was incapable of sitting still. In perpetual motion, hyperactive, tireless, ready to undertake everything and be successful at everything. Unable to grasp that her entourage didn't immediately jump in and embrace her projects as their own. During these manic periods, she was easy to talk to; she sang *Carmen* or *La Traviata* ("What, you don't know it?"); she was voluble; she had a sense of humor . . .

But all these excesses made us anxious, especially as we knew they were invariably followed by crying fits, lamentations, or anger. The slightest vexation made her explode. She would start to yell and scream. What always appalled me—and reinforced me in the conviction I had acquired at age ten that the earth could shake under our feet at any moment—was the suddenness of the tipping point. The smallest thing could irritate her. An innocuous remark, an innocent smile, footprints in the vestibule, breakfast dishes left uncleared, an unmade bed, a mislaid pair of scissors, something she had asked us to do and that had been forgotten even though we had "nothing else to think about" could trigger a fit of rage and an animosity that it would take days to mitigate. When the tipping point occurred, she became unrecognizable. Her eyes flashed with hatred. She could seem raving mad. Her scathing remarks, her irrevocable criticisms pierced the flesh. Her determination to ridicule her interlocutor—usually, my father—left us stunned, speechless, terrorized.

These extreme mood swings were followed by a period of frozen tension. Tense meals during which the pendulum of the dining room clock was the only sound you could hear; no one dared to move a muscle; my sister sighed or cleared her throat; Papa tried in vain to start a conversation that inevitably went nowhere. I will never forget the way my mother looked at those moments, the hard look in her eyes. And then, just like in the mountains, the seracs cracked eventually, the ice broke, and a stream of tears and reproaches poured forth. Despair, the feeling of loneliness set in. No one had ever loved her or understood her. She felt mistreated by everyone. She kept repeating that she was inadequate and worthless. She disparaged herself endlessly.

Only much later did I become aware of the deep mental pain underlying these bouts of sadness and discouragement. Why weren't we told at the time that this was a disease? We had been swept up unknowingly—at least we, her daughters—into the infernal bipolar cycle, manic-depressive psychosis or MDP. Alternating between howls and desolation—with, fortunately, periods of remission. It was impossible to escape from it; in a nutshell we suffered from "passive MDP," akin to what is called "passive smoking." And we blamed her for inexplicably wrecking our lives every day.

For we didn't understand. It was beyond anything we could understand.

A Freedom Too Great for Us

Papa's version was always one and the same: "Your mother is a colorful person. Like everyone, she has her ups and downs, but being Italian, her ups are higher and her downs are lower . . ." Period; that was it; that's as far as it went. He didn't like to talk about it. In fact, in general, he didn't like to talk. He was a meditative, silent person. As time passed, little by little, he too became self-effacing.

Was he right to smooth over the pathological aspect of it? Did he himself want to believe in this story? Did he know all the ins and outs of it? To this day, I have no answers to these questions. Besides, what would my sister and I have done if he had clearly explained to us that we were dealing with a serious disease—which is what we sensed? I guess this would only have shifted the emphasis of the questions. The very questions I'm still asking myself today: How are children affected by their mother's depression? How does it change them? How do they pull through it? And how does it shape the relationship they will later have with their own children?

This childhood, it seems to me, deposited sediment in strata.

At ten and eleven, I was paralyzed with fear. It was a very old anxiety that was, as it were, enclosed in a cyst. When we were still living in Paris, in her periods of nervous exhaustion, my mother used to make a much-dreaded statement: "If you don't calm down immediately, I'm going to pack my suitcase and leave." There was this permanent dread of impending disappearance, the threat of abandonment that I now see as dreadfully violent. Perhaps it heralded the subsequent tipping point—being ill was also a way of leaving.

I remember a sentence I used to repeat to my daughters when they were very little and I had to travel for work. This slightly odd sentence was, "Mothers always come back." I now realize it's the exact equivalent of "I'm going to pack my suitcase and leave." As if I wanted to drum this certainty into them. So that the objective fact of my departure would merge in their minds with the incontrovertible, obvious fact of my return.

Fear. Fear mixed with guilt. After she returned from the clinic, one day my mother repeated a remark made by Dr. B. (Dr. B, who was treating her at the time, was a prominent Paris psychiatrist. I later found out that he had been Romain Gary's doctor—which was not very reassuring.) This famed Dr. B. had declared, "You can go home to your daughters. And tell them they have nothing to do with any of this." His remark had completely baffled me. If he so much as entertained the thought that the presence of children could play a part in the illness, it had to be because he too believed we could be a triggering factor. We weren't *automatically* off the hook. That being the case, nothing prevented us from making a mental list of all the things we could blame ourselves for and that he didn't know about. The guilt was bottomless.

Between ages twelve and fourteen, I do my best. When Mama is in her depressive phase, she is "oppressed." As soon as she wakes up, she is assailed by dark thoughts. An iron cage constricts her chest. She has trouble breathing. In those moments, I am reminded of a verse from Samuel in the book of Kings. A verse that Father Carreau made us recopy in catechism class:

"And it came to pass, when the evil spirit from God was upon Saul, that David took an harp, and played with his hand: so Saul was refreshed, and was well, and the evil spirit departed from him."

Try as I might, though I played the piano, I couldn't save the day. True, it wasn't David's harp. Only Bach's *Inventions* full of wrong notes.

At sixteen, I'm exasperated. On the mornings when I don't have classes, I can't wait for her to go to work, for her to leave for the pharmacy. It's the one thing I look forward to. So I can finally be alone. Her departure is always preceded by a feverish and stressful commotion. She treads up and down the stairs, probably because she has forgotten her gloves or her scarf, taking the opportunity to open the door to my bedroom and exhort me to get up—she doesn't like anyone to waste time in bed. Then she issues a few instructions for the morning: empty the dishwasher; peel the beans; go pick some chamomile in the garden for tonight, and cherries too—they'll be eaten by the birds if we don't pick them today. I make believe I'm asleep. After that, she's downstairs, looking for her keys and getting all worked up. I hear her stampede on the red marble flagstones, the dull, rapid thump of her pumps. The door slams—with a bounce because of the joint that always catches. Turn of the key in the lock. Screeching of tires on the gravel. Silence.

One more paradox. Much later, my sister and I will be affected by the same syndrome. We return from a weekend in Tours where we've just dealt with a crisis. We're both over forty, married with children, and yet for days on end, her screams, her icy voice, her hard gaze, the infinite violence of her temper tantrums never cease to haunt us. As does the suffering that undermines her. All of this preys on us, ties our stomach in knots, never really leaves us.

Yet, in the days when we were adolescent girls, when the door closed and a perfect silence descended on the house, we couldn't help experiencing an inexplicable feeling of emptiness. The sense of nothingness would expand and suddenly take up all the space. This freedom we were being offered for an entire day was too much for us. Like an oversize garment that hung too loose. We had nothing left to rebel against. For a brief time—this is still a bit the case today—we were lost.

Only those who have experienced this mental torture know that it is not exaggerated to compare it to a form of "ordinary" torture. Eventually a strange bond of dependency sets in between the torturer and the prisoner, an intimate bond made of mutual knowledge, not to say "connivance." But in this case, each mother and daughter perceived the other as the torturer and herself as the prisoner.

Her Mother

I barely remember my maternal grandmother. She died when I was eleven.

"It's funny the memories I have of my mother," my own mother said to me one day. "She was a very cheerful woman, she sang all the time, she laughed easily, she was a bit childish at times. And then, all of a sudden, she would sink into despair and dejection. One day, I was twenty years old and a pharmacology student. Coming home from class, I found her lying in the dark, shaking, on the verge of death. She had swallowed three small bottles of phenobarbital-based or barbiturate-based Veriane Buriat. Fortunately I knew the dose limits, I knew how much could be taken daily. When I saw the bottles in the bathroom trash, I ran to the doctor's: 'Mama has committed suicide, Mama has committed suicide.' The doctor told me to run back home and to make some very strong coffee—he would be joining me. We pulled her out of bed, brought her into the toilet, made her vomit over the toilet bowl. We rubbed her to revive her circulation and we put hot-water bottles around her body. She was breathing. We made her drink small quantities of coffee. I watched over her all night; my father wasn't home. When he returned, he said, 'Your mother isn't here?'

"I said, 'She's sick.'

"'Oh, what is it this time?'

"I have no idea what went on between the two of them," my mother said in conclusion, lowering her voice. "But the next day, for the first time in my life I saw my father come home with a bouquet of flowers."

Her Mother's Mother

Of this grandmother, I scarcely have any memory at all and a fortiori I know nothing about her childhood. I hardly sought to know her, in fact—perhaps this was a way of protecting myself, I preferred to find shelter with the other side, the robust and hearty Ardennes branch of the family. Only once, in my presence, did my mother briefly describe the circumstances of her mother's arrival into the world:

"She was born nine or ten months after the death of her older brother, who had fallen out of the window at age two. My grandmother, Adrienne de Vieilletoile—'Oldcloth,' a name you couldn't possibly make up—found she was pregnant two weeks after this tragedy, no doubt sexually assaulted by her husband. My grandmother conceived a bitter hatred for this embryo growing inside her. As well as for the child that was born. She never concealed this fact . . ."

Finally, she added, as if to excuse her, and to excuse herself, the words I had already heard before she expressed them:

"My mother, who was depressive, had good reasons for being so."

Sneaking Away from Myself

The lawyer and me. Our eyes meet. I feel he's addressing another woman. It's not his fault. How could he know that he's referring to a stranger when he uses my legal first name that no longer exists . . .

It was a long time ago. Everyone took it as a whim. A friend even said to me, "It's the absolute transgression. Do you realize that? To reject the first name your parents gave you and choose another one for yourself!" The fact is, at eleven, I changed my first name. I no longer answered to the old one. I pretended not to understand. Spoiled child no doubt, but above all the desire to be someone else. To peel off the old skin that sticks to your skin. To shed it . . . Yesterday, a friend told me about Kierkegaard and his need to have many pseudonyms so as to—he had nice ways of putting it—"exhaust all the 'I's,'" "shorten the distance between him and himself." I wanted to do the exact opposite. I wanted to go into exile far from myself. As far away as possible from the hateful "real me." In secondary school, of course, on papers and exams, and on official documents, it had not been easy. At first I put down two first names. But these first names were not simple; they didn't fit together. The result wasn't an ordinary combination such as Marie-Claire or Anne-Sophie. Rather, the combination was somewhat grotesque like Cunégonde-Gertrude or . . . But I stood my ground. With time, the original first name disappeared and the second one, the one I had chosen, gained acceptance. I had succeeded in sneaking away from myself.

My parents, I have to admit, were perfectly amenable and played the game without flinching. I was proud. I had demonstrated my free will. Decided for myself. Broken a vicious circle, who knows? In short, I had been free, symbolically, and for the first time, at eleven.

But it didn't change anything.

Lethal Dose

It got even worse. Mama continued to disappear for months on end, after which she would return tired, laughing with a laugh that wasn't authentic. Irritated more and more often, and over nothing. She took medications—a lot. I used to discreetly take out the patient information sheets from the kitchen drawer. I would pronounce the names of the molecules in a low voice. Lithium. Iproniazid. Chloral hydrate and venlafaxine. Hydroxyzine dihydrochloride. Chloral hydrate and fluoxetine. Bromazepam. Prazepam. Chloral hydrate and paroxetine . . . All of this was there in a jumble in the dresser. All the things she must have tried one after the other, or sometimes simultaneously.

Under the heading "Preventing recurrent depression," you could read: "The prevention of recurrent depression is aimed at patients who have had at least three major depressive episodes." Under the heading "Undesirable and troublesome side effects":

"headache, insomnia, sleepiness, other sleep disorders, dizziness, anorexia, tiredness, euphoria, momentary abnormal movements (such as tics, trembling . . .), convulsions, agitation, hallucinations, manic reaction (general overexcitement), mental confusion, anxiety, nervousness, panic attacks (symptoms that could also be due to your illness)." Then there was the following short sentence: "In the event of suicidal thoughts, call your doctor." So it was as simple as that. In the event of a school absence, write a note to your teacher. In the event the super is not on the ground floor, look for him in the stairway. In the event of suicidal thoughts, call your doctor. I continued reading. Under the heading "social phobia": "Social anxiety does not stem from excessive timidity; it is a disturbance characterized by avoidance or fear and interferes significantly with professional and social activities, causing marked suffering." Marked but masked—at least in public. For who, among her customers, noticed anything? With patients, she always said the right thing. She smiled. She was well dressed, well groomed. She camouflaged everything so well.

It was an old-style pharmacy, a provincial pharmacy. At the entrance, there was a poster that used to frighten me a bit because it showed the drawing of an artificial leg and the words I read were steeped in misfortune. The poster listed all the equipment available for rental: medical equipment (wheelchairs, lifts for the handicapped, canes, crutches, mechanical beds, anti-bedsore mattresses, atomizers, baby scales, breast pumps . . .) and orthopedic equipment (belts, elastic stockings, corsets, oxygen tanks for respiratory ailments . . .).

There were wood panels on the walls and, throughout, a characteristic and indefinable odor of pharmacy. Except there was also the smell of eau de cologne because of a big demijohn with a faucet, which my sister and I loved to turn, but either it leaked or we didn't know how to close it properly. In this tranquil atmosphere, my mother, with her natural distinction, must have intimidated her customers. She was not from Touraine, not from their world—but a Parisian woman who had come to live in the country: every once in a while they made a point of making her feel an outsider. I think she secretly suffered from this. She went to great lengths to deliver urgent medications at night to the neighboring farms or houses, making light of the effort involved, did favors gladly and advised people who came to see her instead of "going to the doctor's." They trusted her and, indeed, they were not wrong. She had always wanted to be a doctor, but her father had ruled it out—"not a woman's profession."

So the house was jam-packed with medications. She was surely her own best customer. It seemed to me she could easily have swallowed the entire contents of her dispensary every day. I spent years living with this vague apprehension. In the pocket of her smock was the key to the "B box." I didn't exactly know what that was, but I heard about it all the time. She called these drugs the "toxins": the word alone resonated with danger. My mind was hardly at ease knowing she was free to handle these at her own discretion. One day, talking about her Italian roots, she had said—most probably in jest—that her family descended from the Borgias. I threw myself on the dictionary of proper names. Strange to descend from the son of a future pope! As a good Latin, she always laid it on thick, but I found these poisoning stories far from heartening. For Mama loved to make "concoctions" herself, on her workbench, in the back of her shop. She recounted how in ancient times, people would purge "black bile" with thyme, saffron, and hellebore— according to Constantine the African's *De melancholia,* you could also add "a scruple of scammony." I quote this only for the beauty of the terms for I have no idea what they refer to.

My mother liked words too. She had taught me what the "lethal dose" was, the dose that causes death. The words kept running through my head. "Lethal" sounded almost like "level" and I imagined her spread out on the ground.

In Greece, during vacation, there was that gentle hour when, according to her favorite expression, the sea finally became level. Level water. Level *mater*. Without movement, fixed, still . . .

19

ESP

Much later, I happen to come across an article titled "Evaluation of Suicidal Potential or ESP." The article explained:

> What must be taken into account is that melancholic depression always involves an elevated suicidal potential; a noticeable psychomotor slowdown should not, under any circumstances, lead to confidence on the assumption that the patient will lack the strength to attempt suicide. The death wish is constant and permanent, and sometimes the patient views it as necessary retribution or punishment. Attempted suicide can occur at any moment and sometimes in the final stages of depression after a clear-cut clinical improvement.

Bring Me Your Love

At the approach of winter, it would get even worse. We dreaded the shortened days and the lack of sunshine, which perturbed her mood all the more. The lamp that had been sent from Sweden was of no great help. My mother, for that matter, seemed to have tried everything: light therapy, psychotherapy, psychoanalysis . . .

One day—it was about ten years ago—I called from Paris but the phone rang and no one answered. I learned that she had been rushed to a psychiatric institution in the Loir-et-Cher. It was a Saturday in autumn. I left my husband and children in Paris and drove down to the clinic in a château near Chambord.

A brown and gold light shone on the monumental entrance of what was most probably an eighteenth-century building; it had slate roofs, oeils-de-boeuf, and tall windows with inner shutters facing the Loire River. An impression of whiteness emanated from this massive structure, no doubt due to the tufa again. Apparently, this tenderhearted and porous material that hardens in the air, not unlike many of us, was a recurrent image for me. I thought that here, in this clinic, I might discover what Sainte-Beuve happened to call "touching the tufa," "the original bedrock, deep sincerity."

I parked my car under an old cedar tree and, not without some jitteriness, climbed the double staircase leading to the reception hall. There was something pathetic and disquieting in the contrast I sensed between these proud walls and the anguish of the residents. At the top of the stairs, a sign said soberly: PRIVATE INSTITUTION. SPECIALIZED HOSPITALIZATION. PSYCHIATRY.

I found my mother looking lost and weary. I tried very hard to cover up the ordeal it was for me to see her here, among people whose first names she had succeeded in memorizing and whom she greeted as courteously as possible when we saw them—Françoise, a former math teacher with ravaged features, who had come to recover from a severe depression; Gilbert, who thought he was King François I on his way to the Field of the Cloth of Gold (you couldn't meet him in the hallway without his yelling out, "Charles the Fifth cocksucker!"); and many others, whose names I've forgotten, gesticulating, prostrated, suddenly shrieking for no reason, or provoking an altercation with another patient.

I said, "We could go have tea or something?" My mother led me to the cafeteria where, by chance, there was almost no one. Just an old bearded man whose gaze seemed full of doleful questions. His peace of mind seemed reassuring but when he saw us he spat forcefully into his bowl and sent the bowl flying.

We pretended not to notice. My mother said to me, "I'm not crazy but if I stay here, I'll surely become crazy." She was right, I thought. It was *insane*, in the twentieth century, to lock up non-crazy people with crazy people. It was incredibly brutal. And she had to have enormous courage to cope with this given her vulnerable state.

We took a stroll around the château. In the orangery, there was an exhibit of photographs, taken by the patients, on the theme of hands. A hand knitting, a hand holding a cigarette, hands joined in prayer, a hand grasping a coffee cup, hands clasping their owner's folded arms: all these solitary hands were clutching something. And all these tense fingers, with hooked phalanges, you wished you could straighten the fingers one by one so they could slowly relax and the hands could just be hands. Quiet hands that *give* themselves as is. Hands that amount to the weight of a hand.

Later, I was told that manual work, specifically, was "one of the cornerstones of institutional psychotherapy." I only half listened to the doctor who was explaining this to me. He appeared completely convinced of this. He expressed himself unhesitatingly. "Cultural activities workshops are a tool for working out, institutionally, the structuring of communal life." How obvious it seemed; how well stated. "It is a mechanism that helps patients become rewelded to reality and to the rules of group performance and interaction. A mechanism for internal resocialization."

QED. There was nothing to add. I recalled the waterskiing photos. How many ruined years? How many psychiatrists in thirty years? How much loneliness, how much terror? I held out my hand and said, "Thank you." To conclude he said, "I'm satisfied with your mother's progress . . ." This reminded me of the terrific Bukowski short story, "Bring Me Your Love." The doctor, whose name is Jensen, keeps repeating, "Well, well, well . . ." In the end, he says, looking at Gloria, "Well, well, well. I'm really *pleased* with the progress we've made so far . . ." I wondered if, as in this short story, my mother wasn't perfectly sane and whether it wasn't those of us around her who weren't slowly sinking into the bottomless well of madness.

I went back to her room to say good-bye. I wanted to know if she was sleeping well. "You're basically here to rest. Sleep, sleep, sleep . . ." I took her in my arms—something I never did, for which she had criticized me often enough; she used to say I was cold and had a heart of stone. I took her in my arms and I felt as though she had a frame of glass. So very fragile and breakable. There she was before me, tiny and aged, bent over, and I wondered how she had managed to terrorize us so often, my father, my sister, and me.

For the first time I was nostalgic for her manic spells. I would even have preferred to hear her yell and scream.

MDP

It was then that these three letters began to haunt me. I would combine them, making patterns in silly ways. To the point of filling my datebooks and notebooks with them.

Mute Despairing Passage
Pathetic Me Divided
Destruction, Prostration, Mutism

Misrepresentation, Decline, Protest
Prank, Mutilation, Deliverance
Detestation, Prodrome, Mirror

Misery, Disoriented, Pal,
Presage, Menace, Dispatch

In everyday life, and when I was feeling good, it was Malady Dumb Pernicious or, with an irascible and hurried driver, something like Miserable Depraved Prostitute. Whatever the case, the result was the same. Acronyms and acrostics swirled around anarchically in my brain. Foolishly mocking me all the time.

Papa Mama, Deliver us from evil . . .

Filia Dolorosa

I didn't dare talk about it with Stefa or with anyone. I found myself using terms that, even in childhood, I regarded as the epitome of lies and dissimulation. It was easier to say "convalescent home" than "psychiatric clinic." Easier to say, "My mother is very tired these days" than "My mother has been manic-depressive for thirty years."

Might shame be a factor for us, as heirs of that medieval tradition in which "acedia"—like pride and avarice—was one of the capital sins? My Catholic grandmother from the Ardennes never mentioned the subject except through half-finished questions: "And your mother . . . ? It's unfortunate really . . ." Her ellipses lasted for hours. In her "really" you could hear: (1) her permanent disbelief; (2) the fact that, after all, Mama "had everything going for her"—which she never expressed outright, but which only reinforced point number 1; (3) the idea that in her family, "this" did not exist; (4) her concern for her son and for us, her grandchildren. But as for the patient herself, her symptoms, her progress, her suffering, not one word.

Our prejudices make us less lonely. I didn't blame my grandmother, who was really only handing down age-old received ideas: depression isn't an illness, with a bit of willpower you can get over it; depressives are weak, fragile individuals; or, on the contrary, nothing can be done about depression, it can't be cured, etc., etc. In cafés or public places, I always pricked up my ears whenever someone near me uttered the word. Each time, I was sure to overhear a pearl such as, "it's a rich person's illness," "people are either crazy or normal, there's no middle ground in this area," or again, "he studied too much, it drove him crazy" . . . I was always struck by people who condemned the patient's "self-indulgence" regarding treatment. Comments such as "once you start taking this type of medication, you can't do without it." Should a diabetic be ashamed of having a lifelong dependency on insulin?

When I say ashamed, I think of the idea of sin—the so-called sinful sadness that people used to talk about. Shame, blame, incomprehension, resignation, and irritation: no doubt it was in order to avoid being subjected to all that *in addition* that I cloaked the subject in a discreet and prudent veil. Very early on, I had learned—like my mother—to act as if nothing was the matter. To *give* nothing away.

Yet, as far as I'm concerned, I'm fully aware of why I went to great lengths to avoid the issue. Why I added strata of silence between her story and mine. Why I so wanted to keep it at a distance. Once again, I was afraid. Afraid that I had been inoculated with melancholy and that, through me, my daughters might be contaminated. Afraid of the genes and the transmission—like

Kierkegaard, who is said to have renounced paternity in order to put an end to the family curse. Afraid of this odd *gift* and its strange ambivalence. Afraid, lastly, that because of it, what I thought were my choices, my free will, were just shabby illusions.

In actual fact, I refused to see its telltale signs. But, deep down, I was fully aware that the die was cast. My sister and I had already been "contaminated by the illness." Some summers, I trembled at the thought of sending my daughters to the house in Tours. They went nevertheless because the remedy, I believed, would be worse than the illness; I didn't have the courage to tell my mother the truth and I didn't want to inflict yet another wound on her.

So I would throw myself into the preparations for their departure. At the time, I started to make lists. Very long lists.

What Are We Leaving Behind?

As we were leaving the lawyer's office, my sister suggested we take a walk around the village. I thought it was a good idea—for my parents too. I thought that this sort of gift—whose meaning includes the extension and perpetuation of life beyond one's own—is not necessarily an easy or simple act. It requires detaching yourself from what you constructed, from things that had been a part of your life, hence separating yourself from places, objects, memories. It is probably a form of intentional mutilation that can only be soothed through a lengthy period of patience—a lengthy grieving process? You have to accept to take the crucial step and cross over to the other side. I surmised that this brief legal ceremony was also a reminder of their own deaths. They looked a bit out of sorts, the two of them.

We walked by my mother's former pharmacy. The faces in the

village were unfamiliar to me, but it was strange to be just the four of us, the nuclear family, and to see everything again exactly in its place—the city hall, the police station, the long church behind the bushy linden trees. The school buildings were the same. There was a half-erased hopscotch drawing on the pavement. My sister and I began hopping between HEAVEN and EARTH. It was funny, skipping this way to transcendence.

On the square, the Hôtel des Trois Marchands—which as children looked opulent to us—was empty, its tiles whitewashed. The post office had closed down long ago. "And what happened to Mrs. Santeny's grocery store?" my sister asked. "She kept running the store until she was seventy-five," said my mother. "But then she couldn't find anyone to take over. Yet she had earned a living from it: how come there's no one to take over a business that's doing well?"

"Do you remember?" said my sister. "That girl . . . Yes you do . . . At the time it was the talk of the village. The unmarried girl who gave birth—that was a scandal enough!—to a black baby! And to defend herself, she kept telling anyone who was willing to listen, 'I knew it, there was a big black guy whom I used to pass in the street and he used to look at me with a weird expression.'"

This got me thinking about village life again, its aberrations, grudges, jealousies, and its laughable feuds handed down from generation to generation for reasons that are often completely forgotten.

Suddenly, my mother added, "That lady" (she was still talking about Mrs. Santeny) "had lost her husband in the war. She didn't have any children so she adopted a boy from a large family and brought him up all by herself. This was not uncommon in the country, people took children into their homes to unburden the parents. She *gave* herself a lot. She brought him up until he came of age." I wondered what she was trying tell us. Perhaps just about this generous, lost custom? Had the child evaporated in adulthood, leaving behind only the same sort of nothingness that had come after the double extinction of the grocery and its owner? My mother looked pensive. I didn't ask questions.

On the way out of the village, enormous excavations scarred the side of the road. As my sister and I expressed surprise, my father explained that they were building "a big shopping center or something" as well as "an enormous traffic circle" because "this was the latest fad." Up on a man-made hill, a sign had been driven into the ground, THE MUSKETEER GROUP. I envisioned the garage with shopping carts, the bottles of gas (1 deposit + 1 check = a gift stuffed animal, terms listed on the forms available at the cash register), I could see the Musketeers' red banners, fluttering aloft over the moribund land. For all around, the fields of wheat and colza—which we had learned from our middle school teacher, Mr. Millet (I'm giving his name because it's so appropriate), were the "granaries of the Beauce and of the Touraine marshlands"—these fields had been replaced by fallow land. An odd dowry for the generations to come.

I thought: what are we leaving behind?

Metaphor of the Agapanthus

We went home, to the house. With my mother, I took what is called a "look around the garden." It is one of her greatest pleasures: to survey this haven of harmony, which is a little like her floral bastion against anxiety and ugliness. She never walks around it without pruning shears or a weeding hoe, cutting a withered flower or weed here, or uprooting a growth of undesirable hop clover there. She says, "This hop clover, if you don't remove it . . . It's like, here, you see these shoots sprouting up again green and thick, the plant was half-dead. In gardens, as in life, there are dominant species and species that are prepared to wither away easily. And wouldn't you know, as if on purpose, it's always the rarest, most sophisticated ones that are the least sturdy. If I don't take care of this bank, the big yellow daisies will eventually eliminate the irises, while over here the rudbeckias are invading everything."

To talk about the garden, she has her words: to manure, hoe, prune, espalier, take a cutting, bed, repot, pollard, compost, layer . . . And always many stories: the *jussiée* or primrose willow that colonizes the river owes its name to Jussieu, who brought it back from America in the nineteenth century; horsetail has remineralizing virtues and is excellent for the hair; *Psalliota campestris*, a fungus better known as the field mushroom, has been gathered since very ancient times . . .

Every day, she takes "a look around," like a pianist practices scales: it may be an exercise in serenity. There is a certain indefinable sacred quality about this garden: plants bear human traces. She has such tenderness for the jasmine brought back from Greece ("no bigger than this"), the "malvaceous" irises (with mauve highlights), and her grandmother's agapanthuses, which she introduces to me as if they were her old acquaintances! "The last time we went to Juan-les-Pins—it was just before the house was sold—Césarine" (she means Cesarina Costa, her Italian grandmother) "gave me a cutting. Now, imagine, I have seven enormous pots." My eyes glide from the blue scapes to the pretty antique vases of glazed clay. She adds, laughingly, "They're a bit like my patrimony—or I should say matrimony. A pity you didn't see it: this summer, there were at least fifteen heads per pot, it was gorgeous."

She is right. She is giving me an image that is almost too beautiful. In Greek, *agapé* means "love." I tell myself that this flower must embody a particularly hardy and persistent form of attachment in order to survive through generations and keep multiplying. But what fascinates me most is the part we don't see. Above ground, there are the blue umbels bursting with oblong leaves that droop down with the grace of sprayed water. But underground, the mysterious, famous rhizomes hide. They have nothing in common with the hierarchical system of roots. Reread Deleuze: the rhizome is a subterranean stem that connects one random point to another random point. It has "neither beginning nor end but always a middle from which it shoots up and bursts forth." I think of this buried network, the incredible energy of these stems: sources of creative explosion spawning underground a ceaseless proliferation of filiations and ramifications. There can be no agapanthus without a rhizome, of course. But, conversely, "if you let them spread, they fork, become entangled, cross over one another and eventually suffocate the plant," my mother explains. "You must cut, cut with a spade, so the other flowers can find room for themselves."

Obviously, I like this image. Love and suffocation. The link between the dead and the living; the beauty of a flower undermined by an invisible force that may eventually asphyxiate it; and this incredible subterranean proliferation—a source, simultaneously, of energy and destruction, with, at the center, something akin to love, a calyx that can survive only if someone cuts the invisible tie whose purpose is the reproduction of the same, forever and ever.

Donation, Debt

"Taking a look around the garden." For my mother the expression meant exactly that and more. Looking around meant weighing the subject from every angle, as well as forming one body with it, espousing it, exhausting it in a way. Being entirely present, *physically and psychologically*. It was out of the question to take advantage of this stroll to discuss our lives, our evenings out, or even less the Paris social whirl. It has been a long time since she has been interested in this ephemeral, superficial way of life. Imperceptibly, she has been returning to her poplar grove, her trees, her woods, her river. Besides, she does not particularly like her daughters' professions. She finds journalism undistinguished. "With all your diplomas, you could have done anything," she often says to me. And she emphasizes the point, looking me straight in the eyes: "It's true . . ."

I don't know what this "anything" stands for. What I do know is that I always tried to please her. Studies, diplomas, settling down. I had dinner with X, spent the weekend with Y, and Z greeted one of my daughters with a kiss! Big deal. She took no pride in it and she was right.

And suddenly, it looked far worse. We were planted there, before the agapanthuses, and I realized that she saw me as embodying a species of contemporary vacuity: a person who was a mere façade, a Magritte painting with nothing behind it. Someone who thinks of herself as very well informed on worldly affairs but is just mere hollow appearance. Someone who is convinced of having deciphered everything but is actually a gullible fool.

Was I the one who was missing out on things? Was life beyond my understanding of it? Was that what she wanted to make me aware of today? Was that the real *gift*?

Persephone Seeks Demeter

On that day, I mean the day of the gift, I had the impression of not understanding anything and of simultaneously understanding a bit more. The rush of memories reminded me of a story I often told my daughter S. and which she adored, the myth of Demeter and Persephone. I can see us again in Piraeus as the ship we were waiting for arrived from Aegina. It was out of the question to interrupt the story. S., very little then, walked down the gangway, tugging and pulling my shirt, "So why was Persephone lost? Mama, why was she lost?" During the entire crossing and then every evening at bedtime on the island, over and over again, I had to tell her the story of Demeter and Persephone.

I liked to think that perhaps what she so liked about it was precisely the boundless devotion with which the mother went to find her daughter—the ancient and comforting illustration of the fact that "mothers always come back . . ."

Suddenly, it was obvious. My mother and I *were* Demeter and Persephone. Except that Demeter was the one who spent certain months underground—months when Persephone tried her utmost to pull her out of the hell of depression; then periodically Demeter returned to the daylight to fertilize the earth and cultivate her garden—which was when Persephone found buried treasures by her side. In reality, mother and daughter were incessantly seeking each other out: they were locked in a mutual give-and-take.

On that day, I mean the day of the gift, I saw my mother in the autumn sunshine. Her hair was whiter and shinier than ever. Her features relaxed. She exuded a new peace of mind. Self-confidence? Something fragile, but suggesting an inner peace, a respite, a soul laying down its arms. Five years after her last stay in a psychiatric institution, everything seemed brighter. The texture of the air had changed—more serene, more transparent. She showed me the little red acer that she had just planted next to the island of bamboos. And then—and it never failed to annoy me—she quoted the predictable La Fontaine verse: "Now then, build, maybe . . . But to plant?"

There was contentment in her way of saying it. For the first time, I understood that the act of planting was her way of celebrating the victory of life. The discreet joy of having survived.

On that day, the day of the gift, I felt less afraid.

27

To Give and Forgive

"If man were one single thing, he would never suffer." My mother was not one but two. Janus with "twofold knowledge," knowledge of the past and knowledge of the future, the deity of doors that open and shut—doors often slammed shut in our house, because of her fits of rage or the drafts she hated. Dual woman, asthenic and overexcited, catatonic and ultrapowerful, inhibited and creative. In sum, bicephalous, bipolar like the disorder she had transmitted to us—in duplicate, to my sister and me, as if everything worked in twos!

Tails, the feeling of latent death pangs. The imminent fall. The fear of collapse, for to quote Yeats, "Things fall apart; the center cannot hold." Like her, in my inner depths, I have the idea of a gaping openness, an empty space that I can stumble into. From one moment to the next it will swallow me up and I'll disappear inside it.

But when I turn the coin over to heads, oddly, a vital source looms before me, the very essence of things. There is a phrase of Winnicott's: "It is out of non-existence that existence can be born." This is a phrase that Stefa taught me (a good pediatrician, she is a fan of Donald Woods—Winnicott—she sometimes refers to him by his first name as though they were personal acquaintances). What I principally retain from this is the comforting idea that having a different rapport to the world can give rise to creativity; in other words, that there is a great affinity between melancholy and form—or beauty.

So, my mother, without knowing, gave me all of these things in a jumble, the good, the bad, the light, the dark. She gave the A note, setting the tuning for our family relationships. Yes, that was the *given*—in any case, the one I thought I had received and always sought to change. But it was impossible.

I had resented her. I had forgiven her. Forgiven her for having had too many gifts—including the noteworthy one of having wrecked the lives of all four of us. Forgiven our estrangements, our clashes, our moments of incomprehension. By the end of that day, I saw the *gift* as an authentic act of peace inter vivos, as the lawyer might have said. From now on, she and I could be in harmony with the world. *Give* our consent to what we are.

I saw somewhere a list of the great manic depressives of history. To myself, I called them with tenderness "my dear MDPs." Andersen, Churchill, Gauguin, Conrad, Fitzgerald, Poe, T. S. Eliot, Martin Luther: the list was long and served no purpose, absolutely none, except, perhaps, to become reconciled—to what, I don't know. Apparently, one of them said, to never have experienced this illness would have been the gravest affliction of all. This struck me as stupid. Wouldn't things have the same flavor without melancholy's salty tears? What I did know in any case was that this illness was too elusive, too intimately mixed with life, to be a matter for psychiatrists alone.

As for me, I was learning to live with the pain. This archaic, centermost, ineradicable pain. My thought was: I created myself with it, I learned to love it. Learned to love myself *like this*. My thought was, love and melancholy were a bit like the rhizome. No sooner planted, they multiplied, divided, created complex entanglements and deep displacements. The danger of suffocation should not be underestimated. The blunt use of the spade should be kept in mind. And re-create yourself nearby, as not quite different and not quite identical.

Perfect happiness: accepting that happiness doesn't exist.

Dear Parents

As if we were on an airliner about to take off, there was an announcement informing us that we had "boarded train number 3524 with Paris as the final destination." In my car, a group of English visitors were returning from an organized tour of the châteaux de la Loire. Their suitcases bore the label HANDLE WITH CARE. I thought, in English, "Oh, yes, handle with care. And don't touch me, I'm full of tears . . ." (For me, *care* is one of the loveliest words in the English language: "Take care of yourself, will you . . ." Or better yet: "Bear in mind how much I care . . ." Not to mention the mythical "My Baby Just Cares for Me" in the velvety voice of Nina Simone, which I listened to over and over again in a loop on my iPod—it was practically the only song I had along with "I Will Survive;" it feels so good having someone who doesn't give a damn about anything except you and who teaches you how to survive.)

Like a fragile package, I settled comfortably in my seat, and took out my paper and pen again:

> ~~Dear parents,~~
> ~~Just a word to thank you again for~~
> ~~I wanted to tell you how~~

No. This was a unique opportunity to really talk to them. Not just thank them for the gift, but connect the material and the nonmaterial, tell them that my gratitude had come a long way: it had overcome suffering and abandonment, the feeling of loss, the horror of pointless waste, and the bitter rancor of incomprehension. It had followed a long, weary path before breaking forth, in broad daylight, in a lawyer's office. Out the window now, the silhouettes of Beaugency houses flew past, houses with age-old shapes, huddled close together. My thoughts glided over the leaden gray of the slate roofs, when a stream of words suddenly came to me, in a strange, quasi-automatic way.

I wrote—no doubt with Dagerman in mind:

> *We are all orphans. Our need for consolation is insatiable.*
>
> *I was ten years old when I lost my parents. They are both in fine shape today, but I keep moving heaven and earth to recapture something of the life from before. I can't pinpoint what exactly. I'm looking for the original bedrock. A trace from before the world was turned upside down.*

I kept on writing. Very quickly. And very quickly too, the past began to invade the blank pages. A kind of flood out of which everything surfaced pell-mell, my mother's illness, my father's retreat, skipping from one time frame to another, from one state to another, the summer in Lausanne, the idea that life was being played out somewhere else, without me, that I didn't count at all, that I wasn't loved, the "great reunion" on the Riviera, the psychiatrists, clinics, medications, crises, psychodramas, the screaming and yelling, the unvoiced rancor, the insecurity, the constant fear, the fear of everything, the indelible imprint of the primal malaise, and especially, above all, the dread of passing on a wound that came from long ago, so very long ago—from human beings we had never known, and days we had never lived through . . .

I felt it was important to tell my mother that I had understood something of this. That the gift could also symbolize our reconciliation. And appeasement. I wanted to tell her that for me this letter was the start of a conversation between two women who had suffered from one another but whose mutual respect had led to their talking and suddenly "getting along."

I was also telling my mother that I had accepted being like her. That her story was also mine—after all, "it was my childhood and I had only one childhood." And also that I had accepted, as a vital necessity, the idea of family, of the past, of lineage, of legacy—in other words, the idea of the larger *gift* which, in its widest sense, extends beyond us all.

That I was happy, that I wanted to hug them, that I was eager to see them again.

"All I Have Got Is What I Have Not Got"

In Paris, I called Stefa from the bus. I wanted to find out if anything was new, if she had heard from H., and tell her about my little round trip. "Do you realize that you're talking to a 'bare owner'?" With her almost inaudible Prague accent, she asked me what the meaning of "bare owner" was exactly. And then, predictably, she added, "This reminds me of Winnicott. You know, when he talks about transitional objects. He has incredible turns of phrase: 'The real thing is the thing that is not there.' Or, 'The negative . . . is more real than the positive.' Or again, 'All I have got is what I have not got.'"

I said to myself that actually bare ownership was not so bad. We have, yet we have nothing. "All we have got is what we have not got." And nothing prevents us from building on this lack, as in life. In the end, this metaphor suits me, I thought. I'll keep it . . .

An Eight-Gallon-Capacity
Hefty Trash Bag

I hesitated. I was about to hang up when I offered to read pas-
sages of my letter to Stefa. When I finished, there was a long
silence. She cleared her throat and said, "What can I say?" in an
odd tone of voice. Then she exploded. Quite frankly, she couldn't
for the life of her understand what forgiving one's parents could
possibly mean. She found the whole idea obscene. The fact that
they had brought me into the world didn't mean I owed them
everything, but there's a big difference between that and going so
far as to say I "forgive" them . . . How could I be the one to "ab-
solve"? Forgiveness implied a sin or a mistake. And wasn't I the
first person to say that my mother was not at fault? That she had
simply been sick?

I didn't know what to say at that point. I sat in the bus, twisting
the handle of my handbag and staring into space. That evening, I

thought it over; perhaps she was not mistaken. If human relation-ships rested on equivocations and misconceptions, why add more misunderstandings to what was already a misunderstanding?

I took the letter and converted it into tiny confetti, with me-ticulous care. I stuffed the confetti into a kitchen trash bag. An eight-gallon-capacity Hefty trash bag. I knotted the sturdy draw-string at the top tightly and energetically, leaving a mark on my fingers; it was as though I wanted to nip the potentially damaging effects of this bold correspondence in the bud.

Then I called Tours. My father picked up the phone. I spoke to both of them, in turn. I thanked them—thanked them many times, wholeheartedly. Words that I felt were bland and awkward, as usual. But it didn't matter. I told them that these last two days had been wonderful, that I was eager to return, to come back to the house, perhaps for the next holiday, All Saints' Day, and I sent them a big kiss and told them that everyone here sent them love and kisses.

Epilogue

All Saints' Day, 2005.

School holiday. Bronze light.

We're in Tours, my daughters and I.

November 3, the little one, only four years old, is busy with her coloring book in the study.
Later, she will say, "I saw Grandma fly out the window."

On November 3, 2005, at around six-thirty in the evening, my mother threw herself from the tower.

ACKNOWLEDGMENTS

This work of fiction was written at the Villa Marguerite-Yourcenar in Mont-Noir. I would like to thank the Conseil général du Nord for having had faith in me. I am also indebted to the psychoanalysts, psychotherapists, and psychologists whose advice and works were of invaluable help: Daniela Avakian, Maurice Corcos, Lydia Flem, André Green, J.-B. Pontalis, Chantal Rialland, Maryse Vaillant. The exhibit "Melancholie," which was held in Paris in 2005–2006, was a source of great inspiration, as was the book by Yves Hersant, *Melancolies, de l'Antiquité à nos jours* (published by Robert Laffont).

The book contains hints and allusions—exact quotations and deliberately oblique references—to authors from the past and present, including Stig Dagerman, D. W. Winnicott, Hippocrates, Euripides, Sylvia Plath, W. B. Yeats, Gérard de Nerval, Søren Kierkegaard, Henri Calet, François de Malherbe, Jules Supervielle, Ted Hughes, Olivier Adam, Camille Laurens, A. D. du Chatelle, Carlos Liscano. I should like to thank them as well. The article quoted in chapter 12 is by Catherine Petitnicolas (*Le Figaro*, January 17, 2006).

This family portrait is imaginary; any resemblance to living people is purely coincidental.